Franz Liszt

PIANO TRANSCRIPTIONS FROM FRENCH AND ITALIAN OPERAS

Selected and with an Introduction by

Charles Suttoni

Published in association with the
American Liszt Society by
DOVER PUBLICATIONS, INC.
NEW YORK

Published in Canada by General Publishing Company, Ltd., 30 Lesmill Road, Don Mills, Toronto, Ontario.

This Dover edition, first published in 1982 in association with the American Liszt Society, contains selections from the following volumes of *F. Liszt/Opernye transkriptsii dlya fortep'yano* [Piano Transcriptions from Operas], originally published by the Gosudarstvennoe Muzykal'noe Izdatel'stvo [State Music Publishers], Moscow, under the editorship of V. S. Belov and K. S. Sorokin:
From Volume I, Part 1 (1958): *Almira; Don Juan.*
From Volume I, Part 2 (1958): *Robert le Diable.*
From Volume II, Part 1 (1959): *William Tell; Lucia di Lammermoor; Lucia* and *Parisina.*
From Volume II, Part 2 (1962): *Sonnambula; Norma.*
From Volume III, Part 2 (1964): *Rigoletto; Trovatore; Ernani; Faust; Eugene Onegin.*
All headings, footnotes and other indications that originally appeared in Russian have been translated into English specially for the present edition. A new Introduction has been written by Charles Suttoni, who made the selection.

Manufactured in the United States of America
Dover Publications, Inc.
31 East 2nd Street
Mineola, N.Y. 11501

Library of Congress Cataloging in Publication Data

Liszt, Franz, 1811–1886.
  Piano transcriptions from French and Italian operas.

  Selections from Opernye transkriptsii dlia fortep'iano, v. 1–3, by Liszt, edited by V. S. Belov and K. S. Sorokin, published in 1958–1964 by Gos. muzykal'noe izd-vo, Moscow.
  Contents: Almira — Don Juan — Robert le Diable — [etc.]
  1. Piano music.
M22.L77B4   1982   81-15307
ISBN 0-486-24273-0   AACR2

Introduction to the Dover Edition

I

It was perhaps inevitable that opera and the piano would merge their respective arts in the first half of the nineteenth century. Opera was popular musical theater, and each season, much like first-run Broadway musicals, it furnished the public with a spate of new, attractive melodies, familiar themes that the generally unsophisticated audiences of the day also insisted upon hearing in concert.

For its part, the piano was the first solo instrument to rival the orchestra. Each home with a piano became its own opera theater or concert hall since overtures, arias and symphonies could all be transcribed into pianistic terms—the nineteenth-century equivalent of a recording. It was, however, a small but virtually irresistible step from transcribing in a strict, unadorned manner to adding embellishments, which is exactly what pianists of the time did in concert: they took the familiar melodies and improvised on them, wrote sets of variations on them or fashioned them into freely conceived fantasies, often built around several contrasting themes and published with a bewildering diversity of titles, such as Fantasy, Reminiscences or Caprice.

In this same era, the piano itself underwent a number of mechanical improvements. Besides increasing in range from six to seven octaves, it became more responsive, more agile, yet sturdier and more sonorous. Pianists, of course, were quick to explore and exploit the instrument's evolving capabilities. They took particular delight in "the difficulty overcome" by creating new figuration and depths of sound which they promptly displayed in the most popular of their concert works, the opera fantasies. Mendelssohn, for instance, once wrote his sister about Liszt's greatly talented rival Sigismond Thalberg and remarked that "a Fantasia by him is a piling up of the choicest, finest effects and an astounding climax of difficulties and elegances." Liszt, however, was the greatest, the most innovative pianist/composer of them all, and while he sought out new techniques and sounds in all his works, his fantasies merit a special place among them. Brahms, in fact, held the opinion: "Whoever really wants to know what Liszt has done for the piano should study his old operatic fantasies. They represent the classicism of piano technique" (reported by pianist Arthur Friedheim in his memoirs *Life and Liszt*).

In his long career as a composer Liszt (1811–1886) wrote some sixty works based upon popular operas of his day. Not all qualify as fantasies, since many are basically transcriptions —inimitable and idiomatic translations of orchestral language into that of the piano. The operatic transcriptions are mostly late works, while the bravura fantasies quite understandably date from his virtuoso years when, like his contemporaries, Liszt featured his own compositions at his concerts.

Although Liszt the "virtuoso" often dominates our image of him, his active period amounts to barely a decade: from a concert in Vienna for Hungarian flood relief in April 1838 to his final concert in Elizabethgrad in September 1847, after which, at 35, he retired from the concert platform. Prior to his virtuoso travels he had only performed sporadically, mostly in France and Italy. It was in Paris that he had his well-known encounter with Thalberg, a conflict that divided musicians into two acrimonious camps. The young men—both 25 at the time —faced each other in March 1837 at a charity gala where each chose a fantasy as the ideal means of presenting himself: Thalberg his Fantasy on Rossini's *Moses* and Liszt his Divertissement on "I tuoi frequenti palpiti" from Pacini's *Niobe*. Although this contest resulted in the frequently cited ambiguous judgment, "Thalberg is the leading pianist in the world, but Liszt is the only one," it had much deeper implications. Thalberg's style, renowned for its "singing" touch, was serene, self-assured, and his *Moses Fantasy* generated an unprecedented wealth of sound. Liszt's style, by contrast, leaned toward the impetuous and the brilliant.

Liszt learned a great deal from the event and gradually weaned his style away from the emphatic glitter that sometimes mars his early works. Thalberg, unfortunately, learned little. His favorite effect—it occurs in the finale of *Moses*—was to present the melody played by alternate hands in the midst of sweeping arpeggios. At first it so astounded audiences that they would stand up trying to see how it was done, but Thalberg repeated it so often that he was soon dubbed "Old Arpeggio." Liszt, in works such as the *Reminiscences of Norma* and the Concert Etude "Un sospiro," adopted the device and made it his own.

A year after the Thalberg encounter Liszt presented himself to Europe at the Vienna concert for flood relief and promptly sent the musical press into a decade-long scramble for superlatives in its attempt to describe the phenomenal young man and the effect he created on audiences. One renowned piano pedagogue, Friedrich Wieck—together with his daughter, soon to be the famed Clara Schumann—happened to be in Vienna at the time and even he succumbed: "Well, yesterday," he wrote his wife, "we [Clara and I] heard Liszt in concert! And that must be an unforgettable experience for a pianist. . . . His extremely artistic appearance, combined with the highest, most unbelievable mastery of every possible aspect of technique, evoked the stormiest applause." This concert included the Fantasy on Bellini's *Puritani*, but even though it and similar works continued to star at subsequent concerts, Liszt did not confine himself to fantasies. As one of the first pianists to program other composers, he performed works by Weber, Hummel and Beethoven as well as some contemporary works by Chopin and Schumann. He also played his transcriptions: Beethoven's *Pastoral Symphony* was a particular favorite, as were Schubert lieder, Rossini's Overture to *William Tell* and excerpts from Berlioz' *Symphonie Fantastique*. Original pieces — études, the *Grande Valse de Bravura* or the celebrated *Galop Chromatique* — found their place as well. All in addition to the fantasies.

Among these, the *Reminiscences of Robert le Diable* — the *Valse infernale* — probably caused more public commotion than any other piano piece in history. Liszt introduced it to Paris on March 27, 1841 at his first solo recital there. It caused such a sensation that the audience attending a second recital that was not to include *Robert* demanded he play it on the spot. Then came the famous, or notorious, incident at the fund-raising concert, April 25, 1841, for a monument to Beethoven. It was an all-Beethoven program that included Liszt as soloist in the E-flat Concerto (with Berlioz conducting), among other works. The Parisians, nonetheless, again roared out for *Robert* and left Liszt no choice but to perform the bravura work, which "the public," noted a journalist present, "interrupted many times with expressions of enthusiasm, if not delirium." Richard Wagner, also present, was scandalized, commenting in the German press: "One day Liszt, in heaven, will be called upon to play his fantasy on the devil before the assembled company of angels." No matter, though, what Wagner thought: all Paris wanted to see the music, and the day *Robert* was published it sold over 500 copies.

Flushed with the success of *Robert*, Liszt turned quickly to *Sonnambula*, *Norma* and *Don Juan* (*Don Giovanni*). "It is a new manner I have found and want to cultivate," he informed his mistress Marie d'Agoult. "As to effect, these latest works are incomparably superior to my earlier things." Indeed, the four pieces comprise the summit of Liszt's fantasy writing. In each, he has selected his themes carefully so that they present a cogent dramatic point of view: Liszt's personal interpretation, as it were, of each opera. Their stress on thematic connection, moreover, sets them apart from many contemporary works, which were frequently little more than potpourris of favorite but independent melodies.

As to their pianistic and technical effects, one can perhaps second Brahms's opinion by highlighting a few of them. In *Don Juan*, Liszt achieves extraordinary orchestral power in the opening section, and in the duet "Là ci darem la mano" he shows an uncommon sensitivity to the way Mozart had scored the voices of the Don and Zerlina. In *Robert*, melodies presented individually are combined at the climax. This procedure, traditionally known as a "Réunion des thèmes," is an ingenious and audience-pleasing method of enhancing musical

interest. Liszt liked it and put it to good use in a number of fantasies. *Norma* presents a compendium of pianistic figuration in which each type of passage-work seems ideally suited to the character of the theme it supports or embellishes. In addition to its Thalbergian arpeggios, *Norma* also contains one of the most sublime episodes ever conceived for the piano: the B-major episode, *Più lento*, about which Ferruccio Busoni remarked that anyone who fails to be moved by it "has not yet arrived at Liszt." Busoni also felt the same about the B-flat minor *Andante con molto sentimento* in *La Sonnambula*. Besides that suave episode, *Sonnambula* presents the performer with a formidable technical challenge — the climactic combination of themes accompanied by a trill. Once when Liszt played it, the effect was so startling that a listener approached him and earnestly asked to see the sixth finger that rumor maintained he had between his fourth and fifth to play the celebrated trill.

Fantasies such as these provided Liszt with the pianistic arsenal he needed as a virtuoso. With his retirement in 1847, however, that need ceased to exist, so his preoccupation with opera-based works waned as he directed his efforts more to original works. On occasion during the next forty years he did return to opera arrangements, but these works have a different musical orientation. He virtually ceased trying to encompass an entire opera in a single fantasy, concentrating instead on a notable episode, the Quartet from *Rigoletto*, or dances, such as the Waltz from *Faust*. He also turned his attention to Richard Wagner and, as their friendship and association developed, became an outspoken champion of his operas. Two years after his retirement, Liszt not only introduced *Tannhäuser* to Weimar, but transcribed its brilliant Overture for the piano. It was the first of the piano arrangements that Liszt devoted to popularizing Wagner's operas.

Most of Liszt's opera-inspired works after 1847 border on transcriptions, and works of this type continued to serve both performers and the public well into the twentieth century by providing them with opera-based material in convenient form. The more elaborate fantasies, on the other hand, virtually disappeared from concert programs in the latter part of the nineteenth century. Liszt's own retirement was one factor in their demise, but in a broader sense these works had so saturated earlier concert life that the form was overexposed. There was little left for it to say. Coupled with this fact was a profound and far-reaching shift in the concert programming of the time to more "serious" works: Beethoven sonatas, for instance, once thought suitable only for private performance, became repertory staples. The fantasies, as a result, fell into deep disrepute.

In recent years, however, they have begun to reappear in concert and recordings. There is, then, no need to defend them or view them merely as historic souvenirs of a time when the piano was confidently testing its potential. Liszt's operatic fantasies and transcriptions stand on their own — full of familiar melody and brilliant pianism.

II

This volume, spanning Liszt's output from 1835 to 1879, presents a selection of his paraphrases and fantasies on operas written chiefly in the French and Italian traditions. (His complete transcriptions of works by Wagner appear in a separate companion volume.)

Sarabande and Chaconne from Almira (Handel). By subtitling this piece a "concert arrangement" Liszt may mislead some into regarding it as a transcription when, in fact, only the melodies are by Handel: brief dances for Spanish lords and ladies that occur in the opening act of his first opera, *Almira*

(1705). Although Liszt reversed the sequence of the two dances, the varied treatment of them is entirely his own. He composed the work in 1879 (published in 1880) for his English disciple Walter Bache.

Reminiscences of Don Juan [Don Giovanni] (Mozart). This great fantasy was written in 1841, and by calling it *Don Juan*, Liszt may well have been thinking of the work's elaborate and similarly titled production then current at the Paris Opéra. But, whatever its source, the Lisztian vision of *Don Giovanni* (1787) juxtaposes and contrasts three highpoints of the drama. Its opening concentrates on the Don and the slain Commendatore by combining the music of their Act II graveyard scene with that of their awesome confrontation at the opera's climax when the Don is dragged off to Hell. The lyric middle section gives the Don's seductive first-act duet with Zerlina, "Là ci darem la mano," followed by variations, and the Don's Act I aria "Fin ch'han dal vino" provides the brilliant finale. This monumental work has, as Busoni noted, "the almost symbolic significance of a pianistic summit." It was first published in 1843, with a revised edition following in 1877.

Reminiscences of Robert le Diable: Valse infernale (Meyerbeer). A huge success in its day, Meyerbeer's *Robert the Devil* (1831) dramatizes the legendary adventures of the 11th-century duke Robert I of Normandy and his conflict between good and evil: his demon father Bertram zealously plots his damnation, while his saintly mother prays for his redemption. And even though Robert chooses salvation at the last moment, Liszt highlighted the score's demonic aspects in his 1841 fantasy by featuring the hellish waltz sung by Bertram and a cohort of black spirits in Act III, as well as two other prominent melodies. The one in octaves, *Dolce con grazia*, is the Seduction by Gambling from the scandalous third-act ballet in which condemned nuns rise from their graves to tempt Robert with drinking, gambling and wenching. The other, *Marziale tempo giusto*, signals the knights' entrance, "Sonnez, clairons," for the tournament that ends Act II. In addition to its virtuosity, a major feature of this work is the ingenuity with which Liszt combines the various themes.

Overture to William Tell (Rossini). In 1838 Liszt made several visits to Italy where he often attended the Musical Evenings given by Rossini in Milan, and it was then that he transcribed the brilliant Overture to *William Tell* (1829) for piano. He also featured this ingenious piano-score version at his own concerts—playing it in March 1841, for instance, at his first solo recital in Paris—and the score itself was published in 1842.

Reminiscences of Lucia di Lammermoor (Donizetti). Soon after Donizetti's *Lucia* went on stage in 1835, Liszt composed an elaborately protracted fantasy that included both the sextet and the tomb scene. When it was published in 1840, however, the publisher split it into two parts, of which this popular excerpt is the first, independent section—a graceful and resourceful transcription of the famous Sextet "Chi mi frena in tal momento?" to which Liszt has added an introduction and brief cadenzas. As usual in works such as these, he is quite sensitive to the disposition of the voices in the opera and reproduces their tessitura wherever possible.

Concert Waltz on Two Themes from Lucia and Parisina (Donizetti). Although he had already published one virtuoso caprice on these same melodies in 1842, Liszt revised and lightened their presentation radically when he included this spirited concert piece in his *Trois Caprices-Valses* ten years

later. As to the themes, the first is the well-known duet "Verranno a te" from *Lucia* (1835), while the second, entering *Allegro appassionato*, is a second-act duet "Ah! chi veggio?" from *Parisina* (1833) in which Parisina's husband justly accuses her of being unfaithful to him. Love and infidelity may be incongruous dramatic concepts but the melodies are musically compatible and complement each other quite effectively when combined at the waltz's climax.

Grand Concert Fantasy from Sonnambula (Bellini). This lengthy, demanding fantasy centers on the dramatic core, albeit an improbable one, of Bellini's 1831 opera: the sleepwalker Amina innocently strays into a nobleman's bedchamber, only to be discovered there by the suspicious, scandalized villagers. Their first-act chorus "Osservate" furnishes the opening theme, as well as a recurrent quasi-refrain. The next section, the suave *Andante con molto sentimento*, presents the lament by Amina's betrothed Elvino "Tutto è sciolto!" from Act II, and Amina's lively vindication "Ah! non giunge" follows. This coloratura showpiece signals the opera's happy ending but Liszt evidently wanted a nobler tune for his finale so he returned to the Act I quintet-finale "Voglia il cielo," *Più animato*, to close the bravura work. He worked on it 1839–1841, and it was first published the following year.

Reminiscences of Norma (Bellini). In his fantasy on Bellini's *Norma* (1831) Liszt transformed a two-hour masterwork into a fifteen-minute concert piece of comparable dramatic impact. He traces Norma's conflict between her duties as a druid priestess and her emotions as a woman in seven themes, rearranging their sequence slightly to suit his adroit précis of the action. Much like the opera itself, the fantasy's opening sections present the ancient Britons' resistance to their Roman conquerors: "Norma viene," the high priest Oroveso's "Ite sul colle," and the martial chorus "Dell'aura tua profetica." Following these, at the modulation to B minor, Liszt proceeds directly to the opera's closing scenes to present Norma's deeply moving melodies: "Deh! non volerli vittime," "Qual cor tradisti" and "Padre, tu piangi?" Resistance then resurfaces in the animated cry "Guerra! Guerra!," after which the fantasy reaches the climactic peroration of "Padre, tu piangi?," the opera's closing sequence. Liszt composed the work in 1841 (published in 1844) and dedicated it to Marie Pleyel, an outstanding pianist who had asked him for an especially brilliant concert piece.

Concert Paraphrase of Rigoletto; "Miserere" from Trovatore; Concert Paraphrase of Ernani (Verdi). Although the *Ernani* piece had its origins in 1849 or earlier, all three of these Verdi paraphrases were completed in 1859 for a series of concerts that pianist-conductor Hans von Bülow was giving at the time in Berlin. In each, Liszt selects one memorable episode and provides it with an introduction and coda. From *Rigoletto* (1851) it is the famous quartet "Bella figlia dell'amore" in the final act; from *Il Trovatore* (1853) the ensemble "Miserere" in Act IV; and from *Ernani* (1844) Don Carlo's moving paean to the dead Charlemagne "O sommo Carlo" in Act III. All three works were published together as the *Liszt-Verdi Album* in 1860.

Waltz from Faust, Concert Paraphrase (Gounod). This piece, completed in 1861 and published within the year, is an extended paraphrase of the waltz scene that ends the opening act of Gounod's *Faust* (1859). During the scene Faust accosts Marguerite for the first time (their verbal exchange is printed in the music), and Liszt then protracts the meeting with a musical leap to the climax of their second-act love duet "O nuit d'amour!" By doing so, he fashions a substantial lyric episode to balance the waltz-derived sections that open and close the work.

Polonaise from Eugene Onegin (Tchaikovsky). Liszt completed this piece in 1879, just months after the opera's premiere. Essentially, it is an expert transcription of the glittering ball scene in Prince Gremin's palace that opens the final act. In it Liszt naturally maintains Tchaikovsky's contrast between the brilliantly realized outer sections of the dance and the more restrained, suaver tone of the central episode.

Charles Suttoni

New York City
August 1981

Contents

page

Sarabande and Chaconne from Almira, Concert Arrangement (Handel)   1
[Sarabande und Chaconne aus dem Singspiel "Almira"]

Reminiscences of Don Juan [Don Giovanni] (Mozart)   18
[Réminiscences de "Don Juan"]

Reminiscences of Robert le Diable: Valse Infernale (Meyerbeer)   51
[Réminiscences de "Robert le diable"/Valse Infernale]

Overture to William Tell (Rossini)   73
[Ouverture de l'Opéra Guillaume Tell]

Reminiscences of Lucia di Lammermoor (Donizetti)   102
[Réminiscences de Lucia de Lammermoor/Fantaisie dramatique]

Concert Waltz on Two Themes from Lucia and Parisina (Donizetti)   112
[Valse de concert sur deux Motifs de Lucia et Parisina]

Grand Concert Fantasy from Sonnambula (Bellini)   129
[Grosse Concert-Fantaisie aus der Oper Sonnambula]

Reminiscences of Norma (Bellini)   152
[Réminiscences de Norma/Grande Fantaisie]

Concert Paraphrase of Rigoletto (Verdi)   174
[Rigoletto/Oper von Verdi/Concert-Paraphrase]

"Miserere" from Trovatore (Verdi)   187
[Miserere aus "Trovatore" von Verdi/Concert-Paraphrase]

Concert Paraphrase of Ernani (Verdi)   202
[Ernani/Oper von Verdi/Concert-Paraphrase]

Waltz from Faust, Concert Paraphrase (Gounod)   214
[Valse de l'Opéra "Faust" de Gounod/Paraphrase de Concert]

Polonaise from Eugene Onegin (Tchaikovsky)   234
[Polonaise aus Tschaikowskys Oper "Jewgeny Onegin"]

Sarabande and Chaconne from *Almira,*
Concert Arrangement (Handel)

2 *Almira* (Handel): Sarabande and Chaconne

4　*Almira* (Handel): Sarabande and Chaconne

6　*Almira* (Handel): Sarabande and Chaconne

*) For an optional cut, skip to the Chaconne, p. 11 [Liszt's note].

Almira (Handel): Sarabande and Chaconne

10 *Almira* (Handel): Sarabande and Chaconne

Allegretto

*See note p. 8.

Almira (Handel): Sarabande and Chaconne

14 *Almira* (Handel): Sarabande and Chaconne

16 *Almira* (Handel): Sarabande and Chaconne

Reminiscences of *Don Juan [Don Giovanni]* (Mozart)

Don Giovanni (Mozart): Reminiscences

*) Skip to the sign ⊕ at top of p. 23, *Andantino* [Liszt's note]. That is, to the second beat of the bar.

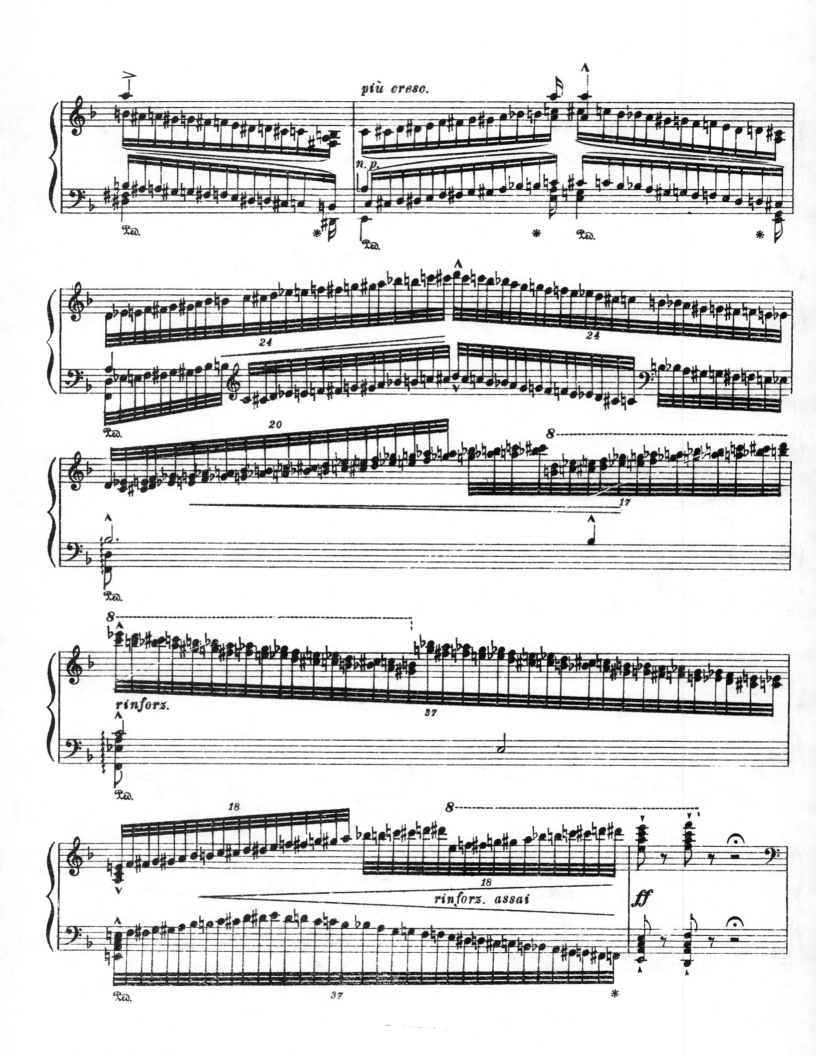

22   *Don Giovanni* (Mozart): Reminiscences

*) See note, p. 21.

24 *Don Giovanni* (Mozart): Reminiscences

Don Giovanni (Mozart): Reminiscences

36   *Don Giovanni* (Mozart): Reminiscences

*) To perform the alternate version, skip to p. 42, bypassing p. 41 entirely.

Presto spiritoso

poco cresc.

poco rit.

lungo trillo

smorz.

*) When performing this version, skip to the sign ⊕ on p. 45, *Presto* [Liszt's note].

42   *Don Giovanni* (Mozart): Reminiscences

44　*Don Giovanni* (Mozart): Reminiscences

*) For an optional cut, skip to the sign ⊕ below [Liszt's note].

+) For an optional cut (?), skip to the sign ✛ below. Both the first (1843) and revised (1877) editions of the work include the signs but no note as to a possible cut at this point [C. S.].

Reminiscences of *Robert le Diable:*
Valse infernale (Meyerbeer)

Robert le Diable (Meyerbeer): Reminiscences

Robert le Diable (Meyerbeer): Reminiscences

Marziale tempo giusto

Easier alternative:

*) For an optional cut, skip to the sign ⊕ on p. 69, *Tempo deciso* [Liszt's note].

*) See note, p. 67.

Overture to *William Tell* (Rossini)

Version for a 6-octave piano:

Allegro (♩=108)

78   *William Tell* (Rossini): Overture

or:

or:

84   *William Tell* (Rossini): Overture

William Tell (Rossini): Overture

94   *William Tell* (Rossini): Overture

or:

100   *William Tell* (Rossini): Overture

*) The presence of a barline is understood here [Editors].

Reminiscences of *Lucia di Lammermoor* (Donizetti)

*) The trill must continue for the full value of the note [Liszt's note].

Lucia di Lammermoor (Donizetti): Reminiscences

Lucia di Lammermoor (Donizetti): Reminiscences

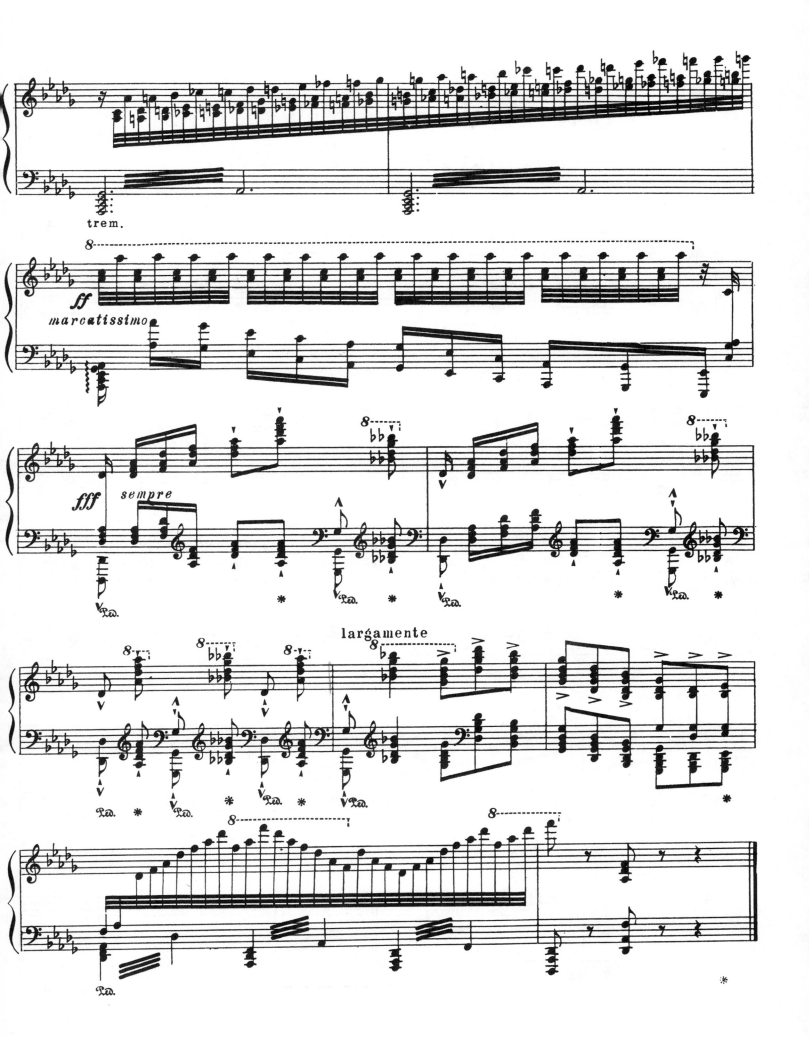

Concert Waltz on Two Themes from
Lucia and *Parisina* (Donizetti)

Lucia and *Parisina* (Donizetti): Concert Waltz

116 *Lucia* and *Parisina* (Donizetti): Concert Waltz

Lucia and *Parisina* (Donizetti): Concert Waltz

Allegro appassionato

Lucia and *Parisina* (Donizetti): Concert Waltz

122 *Lucia* and *Parisina* (Donizetti): Concert Waltz

Lucia and *Parisina* (Donizetti): Concert Waltz

126   *Lucia* and *Parisina* (Donizetti): Concert Waltz

128 *Lucia* and *Parisina* (Donizetti): Concert Waltz

Grand Concert Fantasy from *Sonnambula* (Bellini)

*) For an optional cut, skip to the sign ⊕ on p. 133 [Liszt's note].

•) See note, p. 130.

Sonnambula (Bellini): Grand Concert Fantasy

*) Notes with upward stems are to be played by the right hand, those with downward stems by the left [Liszt's note], referring to the melody in the middle staff.

Sonnambula (Bellini): Grand Concert Fantasy

148   *Sonnambula* (Bellini): Grand Concert Fantasy

Reminiscences of *Norma* (Bellini)

154 *Norma* (Bellini): Reminiscences

Norma (Bellini): Reminiscences

*) For an optional cut, skip to the sign $\oplus$ on p. 167, *Molto più animato* [Liszt's note].

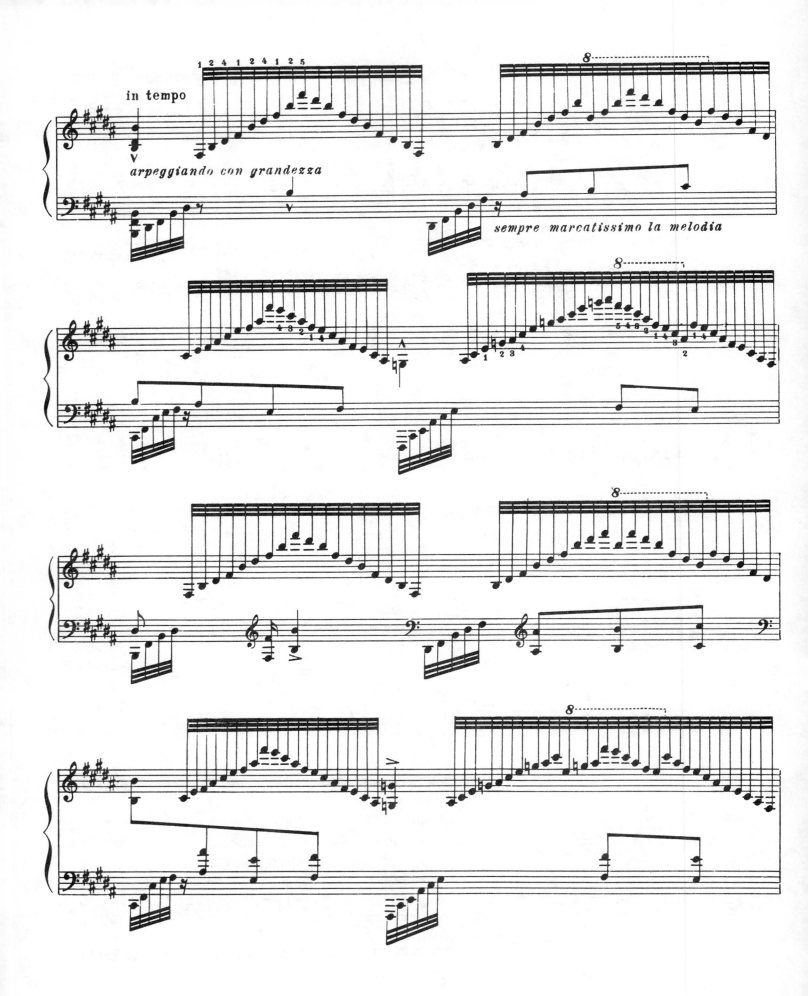

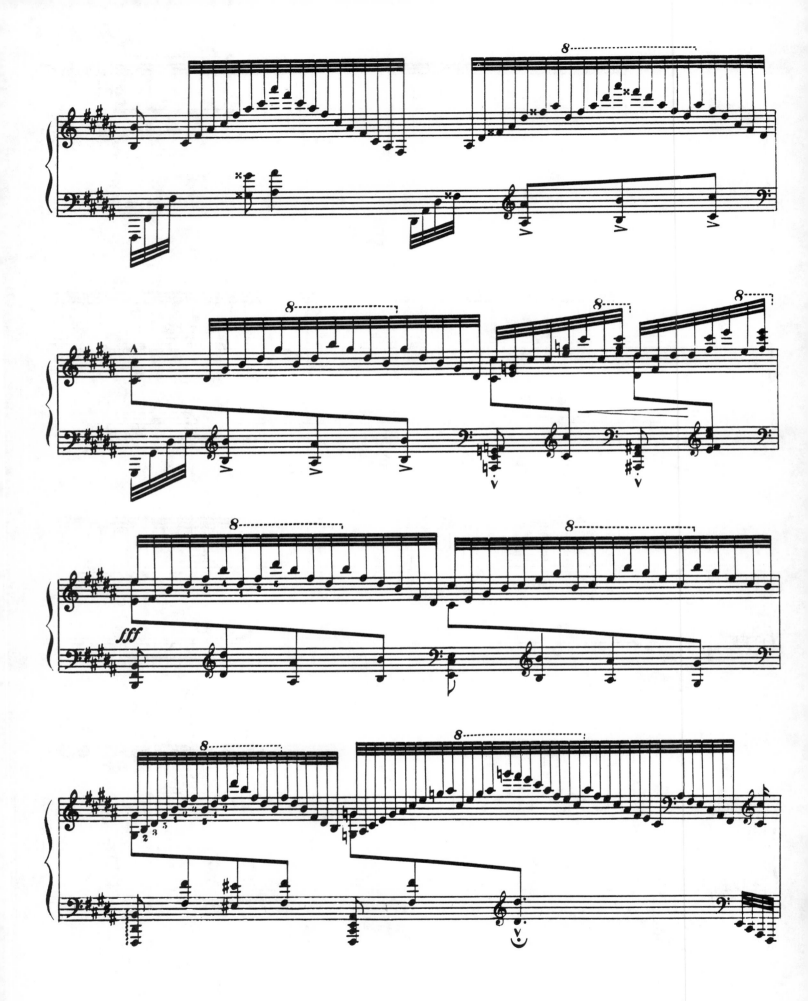

166   *Norma* (Bellini): Reminiscences

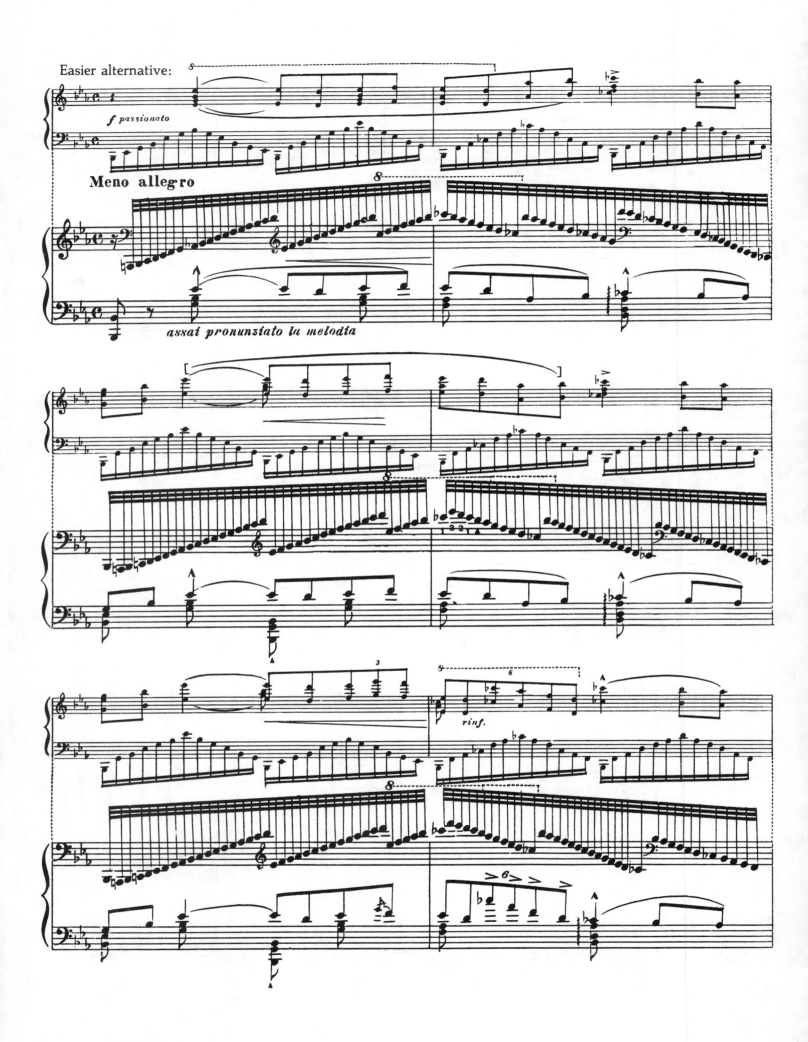

172   *Norma* (Bellini): Reminiscences

Concert Paraphrase of *Rigoletto* (Verdi)

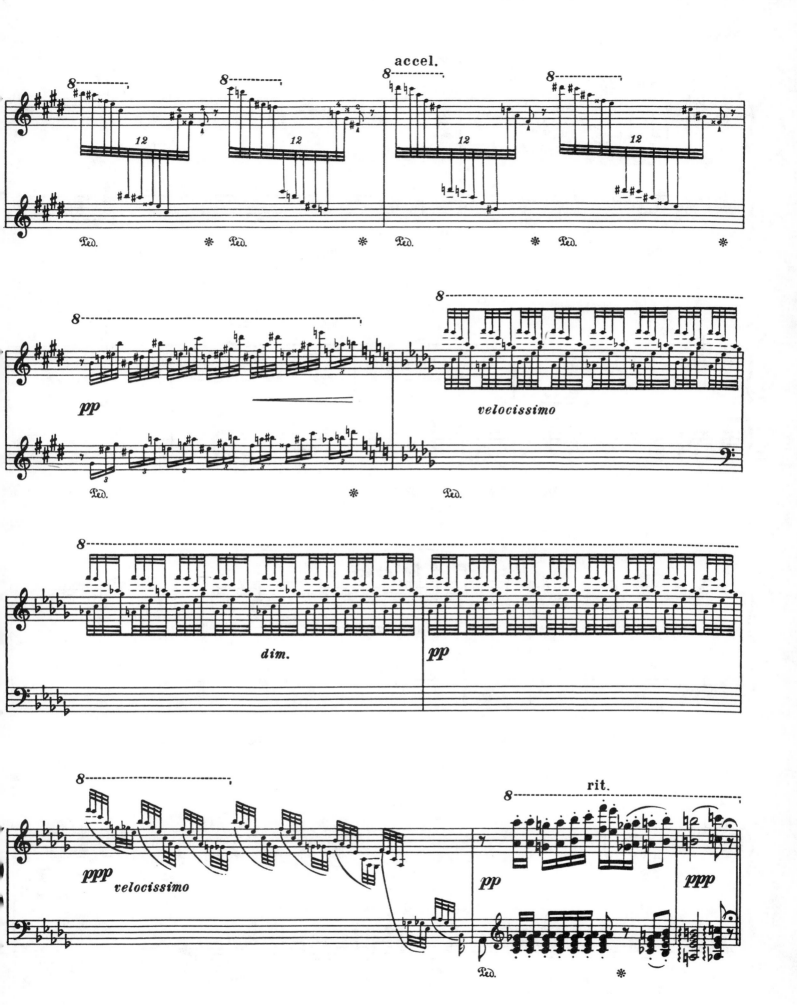

Rigoletto (Verdi): Concert Paraphrase

Rigoletto (Verdi): Concert Paraphrase

"Miserere" from *Trovatore* (Verdi)

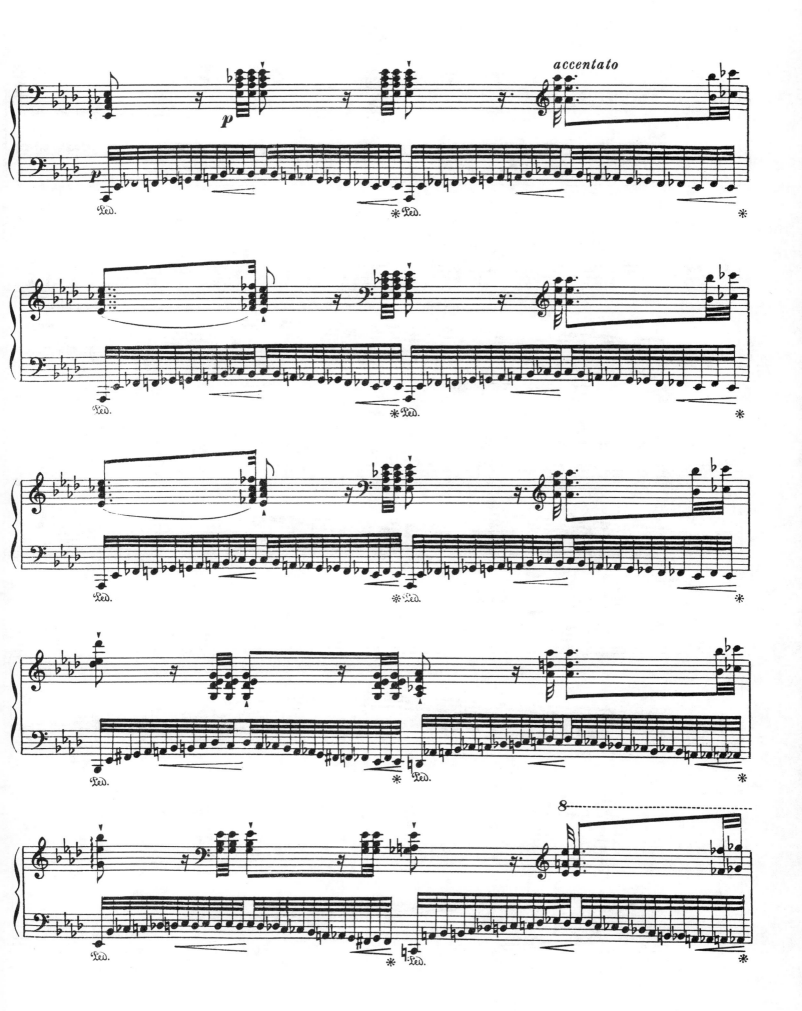

192 *Trovatore* (Verdi): "Miserere"

Pedale 4 fois à chaque mesure

198   Trovatore (Verdi): "Miserere"

Concert Paraphrase of *Ernani* (Verdi)

Ernani (Verdi): Concert Paraphrase

Ernani (Verdi): Concert Paraphrase

Waltz from *Faust*, Concert Paraphrase (Gounod)

216 *Faust* (Gounod): Waltz

*) Skip to the sign ⊕ , *Presto* [Liszt's note].

Faust: „Ne permettez-vous pas, ma belle demoiselle
Qu'on vous offre le bras, pour aller le chemin?"

Marguerite: „Non, Monsieur, je ne suis demoiselle, ni belle
Et je n'ai pas besoin, qu'on me donne le bras."

*) Skip to the sign on p. 225, *Allegro vivace assai* [Liszt's note]. The cadenza version continues and cannot be cut.

*) See note, p. 224.

Faust (Gounod): Waltz

*) Skip to the *Stretta* [Presto] on p. 231 [Liszt's note].

Polonaise from *Eugene Onegin* (Tchaikovsky)

Eugene Onegin (Tchaikovsky): Polonaise

Eugene Onegin (Tchaikovsky): Polonaise

Eugene Onegin (Tchaikovsky): Polonaise

Eugene Onegin (Tchaikovsky): Polonaise